D1152580

TALES OF
ADVENTUROUS
GIRLS

LEVEL

1

RETOLD BY FIONA MACKENZIE AND FIONA MAUCHLINE
ILLUSTRATED BY MOLLEY MAY, KERRY HYNDMAN,
HANNAH TOLSON AND HANNAH PECK

529 890 89 0

PENGUIN BOOKS

UK | USA | Canada | Ireland | Australia
India | New Zealand | South Africa

Penguin Books is part of the Penguin Random House group of companies
whose addresses can be found at global.penguinrandomhouse.com.
www.penguin.co.uk www.puffin.co.uk www.ladybird.co.uk

 Penguin
Random House
UK

Ladybird Tales of Adventurous Girls first published by Ladybird Books Ltd, 2018
This Penguin Readers edition published 2019
001

Printed in China

A CIP catalogue record for this book is available from the British Library

ISBN: 978-0-241-39798-5

All correspondence to:
Penguin Books
Penguin Random House Children's
80 Strand, London WC2R 0RL

MIX
Paper from
responsible sources
FSC
www.fsc.org   FSC® C009967

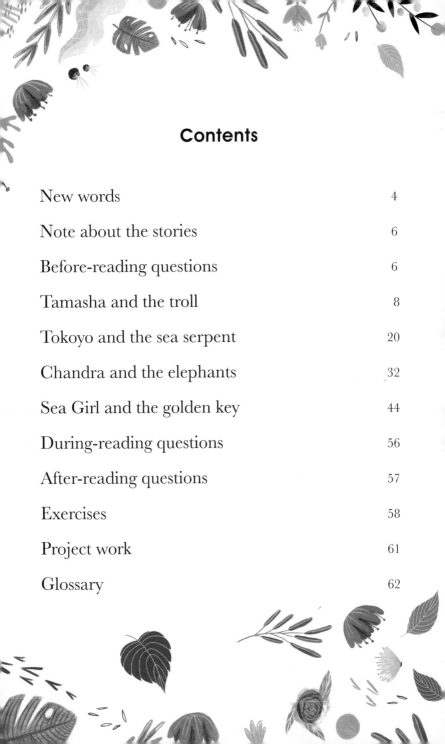

Contents

New words

Tamasha and the **troll**

shell

rock

troll

drum

bees

Tokoyo and the **sea** **serpent**

samurai

Emperor

bow and arrow

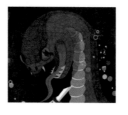
serpent

statue

4

Chandra and the elephants

Rajah

elephant

rice (grain of rice)

board

square

Sea Girl and the golden key

mountain

lake

key

cave

Note about the stories

Girls in fairy stories are often very beautiful and wear beautiful clothes, but they are not **adventurous***. Their fathers, brothers and husbands go out and do **dangerous** things, but the girls wait for them at home.

The girls in these four fairy stories come from different places. They come from Zanzibar, Japan, India and China, but they are all the same. They help their families, friends and animals. Sometimes, the world is dangerous, but these girls are adventurous and **brave**.

Before-reading questions

1 Look at the cover of the book. What are the stories about, do you think? Write your answer in your notebook.

2 Read the back cover of the book. Which of these sentences are true, do you think? Write your answer in your notebook.
   a The book is about girls in their homes.
   b The book is about brave girls.
   c The book is about brave men and boys.
   d The book is about girls in England.
   e The book is about girls in different countries.

3 Make two lists in your notebook with the words from the "New words" pages. You can call the lists "Words I know" and "Words I must learn".

*Definitions of words in **bold** can be found in the glossary on pages 62–63.

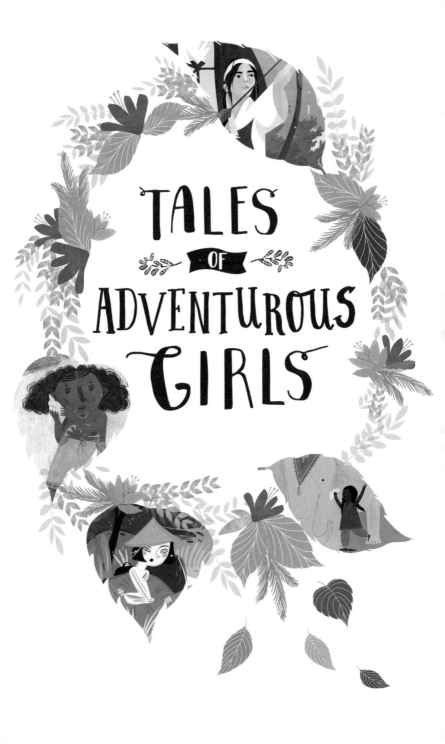

TALES
OF
ADVENTUROUS GIRLS

Tamasha
and the troll

Tamasha lived with her mother and two sisters on the beautiful **island** of Zanzibar.

One day, the sisters went to the beach, and Tamasha found a beautiful white shell. She **held** it near to her ear. "Oh! I can hear the sea!" she thought. Then she sang the song of the sea.

In the evening, the sisters walked home.

"Oh! I forgot my shell!" Tamasha **cried**. Then she ran back to the beach. Her sisters did not go with her.

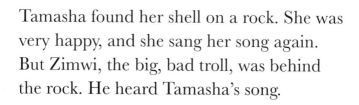

Tamasha found her shell on a rock. She was very happy, and she sang her song again. But Zimwi, the big, bad troll, was behind the rock. He heard Tamasha's song.

"You can sing very well," he said. "You can help me."

Zimwi had a big drum, and he put Tamasha inside it.

Zimwi hit the drum. "Now you must sing!" he cried.

Tamasha sang her song inside the drum.

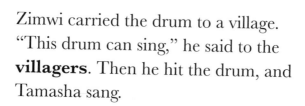

Zimwi carried the drum to a village.
"This drum can sing," he said to the
villagers. Then he hit the drum, and
Tamasha sang.

"Now **bring** me some food!" he cried.

The villagers liked the song, and they
brought Zimwi lots of food.

Zimwi carried the drum to lots of villages.
"Sing, drum," he always said. Then he hit it,
and Tamasha sang. But Zimwi never listened
to her songs.

The villagers gave Zimwi lots of food, but Tamasha was very sad.

One day, Zimwi **visited** Tamasha's village. Tamasha heard her mother's **voice**.

"Sing, drum!" cried Zimwi. Then he hit the drum.

Tamasha sang, "Mother, I'm inside the drum."

"It's Tamasha!" thought her mother. "We must help her!"

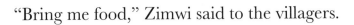

"Bring me food," Zimwi said to the villagers.

"I can cook you some food," said Tamasha's mother. "But I need some water from the river."

Zimwi went to the river.

Tamasha's mother opened the drum and found Tamasha.

Tamasha's mother was very angry with Zimwi. Then she had an **idea**. She caught some bees and put them in the drum.

Zimwi brought back some water from the river.

"Play your drum again!" the villagers cried.

"Sing, drum!" said Zimwi. Then he hit it.

But the drum did not sing. Zimwi hit it
again. "SING!" he cried.

Then the drum opened, and the bees flew
out of it. The bees were angry, and they
flew towards Zimwi. "Ahhh!" he cried.

Zimwi ran out of the village. Tamasha and
her family never saw him again.

Tokoyo and the sea serpent

Tokoyo's father was the Emperor of Japan's favourite samurai. The samurai loved his daughter, and she loved him.

Tokoyo's father was a good teacher.

He taught her how to swim, and how to use a knife, and a bow and arrow.

One day, Tokoyo's father visited the
Emperor, but the Emperor was **confused**.
He was confused because he was **ill**.

"Go to the island of Oki, and don't come
back!" the Emperor told Tokoyo's father.

The samurai went to Oki, and Tokoyo cried
every day.

Then, Tokoyo thought, "I must find Father."

Tokoyo travelled for many weeks. One day,
she saw the sea, and the island of Oki.

There was a village near the sea.

"Please take me to the island," Tokoyo said to the villagers.

"No," they said. "We're **frightened** of the sea because a serpent lives there."

Tokoyo found an old boat. Voices from the sea cried, "Go back!" But Tokoyo was **brave**, and she went to Oki in the boat.

Then she saw a man and a girl at the top of a cliff. The girl was very frightened.

Tokoyo ran to the cliff.

"Why are you in this **dangerous** place?" she cried.

"I must **throw** the girl in the sea," said the man. "Every year, we have to throw a girl to the serpent. Then it doesn't kill people in our village."

Tokoyo was angry. "I can kill the serpent!" she cried.

Tokoyo carried her knife in her mouth, and she swam to the **bottom** of the sea. She found a statue of the Emperor, and she found the serpent.

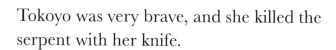

Tokoyo was very brave, and she killed the serpent with her knife.

She took the serpent's body to the man and the girl.

"You helped us," said the girl. "How can we help you?"

"Please find my father," said Tokoyo. "The Emperor sent him to Oki."

The girl smiled. "Your father is living in our village," she said, and she took Tokoyo to him.

Tokoyo and her father went home.

"The Emperor is well now," people said.

"Then let's visit him," said Tokoyo's father.

The Emperor smiled at them. Then he said, "What is that?"

"I killed a serpent, and I found this statue of you," said Tokoyo.

"There was a **curse** on that statue. I am well because you killed the serpent and found that statue," said the Emperor. "You are brave, Tokoyo. You can be a samurai now!"

Tokoyo and her father were very happy.

Chandra
and the **elephants**

Chandra lived with her parents in a village
in India. She washed the Rajah's elephants
every day. She loved the elephants, and they
loved her.

The villagers **grew** rice. Chandra's mother
and father grew rice, too.

"I can help you," said the Rajah to the
villagers. "Let me **look after** your rice."

The villagers brought their rice to him.

One year, it did not rain, and the villagers
did not have any food.

"Can we have our rice?" they asked the
Rajah.

"No!" said the **greedy** Rajah.

The villagers were hungry, but Chandra did
not stop working. She washed the elephants
every day.

But, one day, the Rajah's **guards** said, "You
can't wash the elephants today. They are
very ill."

Chandra was **worried**. "Can I talk to the Rajah, please?" she asked.

The guards took her to the Rajah in his beautiful **palace**. In front of him was a board with black and white squares.

"What do you want, little girl?" he said.

"I'm Chandra. I wash your elephants," she said. "I can help them. Please can I see them?"

"Yes, you can," said the Rajah.

The guards took Chandra to the elephants, and the big animals walked slowly towards her.

"Oh! You are very ill!" said Chandra, sadly. Then she looked at their bodies.

"Oh!" she said. "Your ears **hurt**! I must clean them."

Chandra cleaned the elephants' ears, and, after three days, the elephants were well again.

The Rajah was very happy. "Thank you. What can I give you?" he asked.

Chandra thought about the hungry villagers. "You can give me some rice," she said.

"Of course. How much rice do you want?" asked the Rajah.

Chandra looked at the Rajah's board.

"Please put one grain of rice on the first square," she said. "Then put two grains of rice on the second square, and put four grains on the third square."

"I understand," said the Rajah. "We must **double** the number of grains on every square. Let's start."

The Rajah's guards put all the rice in the palace on the board. Then the Rajah was worried. "There are sixty-four squares. I can't put rice on all the squares," he said. "That is too much rice! What can I do?"

Chandra smiled at him. "You've got the villagers' rice," she said. "Give it back to them."

"Of course," said the Rajah, and he was never greedy again.

Sea Girl and the golden key

Sea Girl lived in a small village near a big mountain in China. Sometimes, it did not rain, and the villagers' rice did not grow.

"I must help my family," Sea Girl thought.

One day, she found a beautiful lake on the mountain.

"We need water," Sea Girl thought. "There is lots of water in this lake."

Then she looked at the rocks next to the lake.

"We can't take this water **down** the mountain," she thought, sadly. "These rocks are too big."

Then she saw a door in the rocks, and she had an idea. "The lake is behind the door," she thought. "I must open the door."

A white bird flew near her. "You must find the key for the door," it said.

"Where can I find the key?" cried Sea Girl.

But the white bird **flew away**.

Then a red bird spoke to her. "You must speak to the Dragon King's daughter," it said.

"Where can I find her?" cried Sea Girl.

But the red bird flew away.

A blue bird stood near her. "Sing! The Dragon King's daughter loves songs," it said.

Then it flew away.

Sea Girl sang two songs. Then a girl walked out of the lake.

"Your songs are beautiful!" the girl said.

"Thank you," said Sea Girl. "Are you the Dragon King's daughter?"

"Yes," said the girl. "Who are you? Why are you here?"

"I'm Sea Girl, and I need water from this lake for my village," said Sea Girl. "Can you help me?"

"Yes, I can," said the girl.

"You can open the door to the lake with my father's key," said the girl. "It's in his cave, but a grey bird **guards** the cave."

The two girls went to the Dragon King's cave. The grey bird sat on a rock near it.

"The bird likes songs," said the girl. "I must sing to it."

The girl sang songs for the grey bird, and it moved towards her.

Sea Girl ran into the cave, and she found the key in a small brown box. Then the girls ran away.

The girls opened the door with the key, and the water went down the mountain.

Now there was a beautiful little river in the village. The villagers' rice grew, and no one was hungry again.

During-reading questions

Write the answers to these questions in your notebook.

TAMASHA AND THE TROLL

1 Where does Tamasha go with her sisters?
2 Where does Zimwi put Tamasha?
3 Why do the villagers bring Zimwi food?
4 How does Tamasha's mother find Tamasha?
5 Why is Tamasha's mother angry with Zimwi, do you think?
6 What do the bees do, and what does Zimwi do then?

TOKOYO AND THE SEA SERPENT

1 Who is the Emperor of Japan's favourite samurai?
2 Why does the Emperor of Japan send Tokoyo's father to Oki?
3 The villagers do not want to take Tokoyo to Oki. Why?
4 What must the villagers do every year? Why?
5 What does Tokoyo find at the bottom of the sea?
6 How does Tokoyo kill the serpent?
7 Why does the Emperor of Japan say to Tokoyo, "You can be a samurai now!"?

CHANDRA AND THE ELEPHANTS

1 What does Chandra do every day?
2 Why does the Rajah look after the villagers' rice, do you think?
3 Why does Chandra speak to the Rajah?
4 Chandra says, "I must clean them." Why does she say this about the elephants' ears?
5 How much rice does Chandra want from the Rajah?
6 What does the Rajah do at the end of the story?

1 The villagers' rice does not grow. Why?

2 Why is the door in the rocks important?

3 Three birds speak to Sea Girl. What do they say?

4 Who is the girl from the lake?

5 Why does the grey bird move away from the cave?

6 Why was no one hungry again in Sea Girl's village?

After-reading questions

1 Here are Tamasha, Tokoyo, Chandra and Sea Girl at the
   end of their stories. What do they say to their families, do
   you think? Draw four big speech bubbles in your notebook,
   and write a sentence in each bubble.

Tamasha   Tokoyo   Chandra   Sea Girl

2 Look at your lists from "Before-reading question 3". Write a
   sentence about each word on your "Words I must learn" list.

3 How are the four girls brave?

4 What is the same in each of the stories? What is different?

Exercises

1 Complete these sentences in your notebook, using the words from the box.

Zanzibar	bees	voice	shell	villages	water

1 Tamasha lives on the island of ....*Zanzibar*..........
2 Tamasha finds a .... on the beach.
3 Zimwi takes his drum to different ....
4 Tamasha hears her mother's .... in her village.
5 Zimwi brings back some .... from the river.
6 Tamasha's mother puts some .... in Zimwi's drum.

2 Complete these sentences in your notebook, using *and*, *because* or *but*.

1 Tamasha found a beautiful white shell, ...*and*.......... she held it near to her ear.
2 Tamasha ran back to the beach, ... her sisters did not go with her.
3 Tamasha sang .... Zimwi hit the drum.
4 Tamasha sang to her mother, ... Zimwi did not listen to her song.
5 Tamasha's mother put some bees inside Zimwi's drum .... she was very angry with him.
6 Zimwi ran out of the village, ... Tamasha never saw him again.

TOKOYO AND THE SEA SERPENT

3 **Write the correct answers in your notebook.**

1 Tokoyo's father was not .....*an emperor*......

   a an emperor

   b a samurai

   c a good teacher

2 When she is travelling, Tokoyo does not see ....

   a the island of Oki

   b the sea

   c the Emperor

3 On top of a cliff, Tokoyo does not see ....

   a a girl

   b some voices

   c a man

4 At the bottom of the sea, Tokoyo does not find ....

   a a serpent

   b her father

   c a statue

4 **Write the correct question words in your notebook.**

1 ....*Where*......... does Tokoyo's father go?

2 .... does Tokoyo see after many weeks?

3 .... are the villagers frightened of the sea?

4 .... many people does Tokoyo see at the top of a cliff?

5 .... does Tokoyo do to the serpent?

6 .... says, "You are brave, Tokoyo."?

CHANDRA AND THE ELEPHANTS

5 Are these sentences *true* or *false*? Write the answers in your notebook.

1 Chandra loves the Rajah's elephants. ....*true*............

2 The Rajah is nice to the hungry villagers.

3 The Rajah lives in a palace.

4 Chandra hurts the elephants.

5 The Rajah has the villagers' rice at the end of the story.

6 Complete these sentences in your notebook. Use the correct forms of the verbs in brackets.

Chandra ¹............*lived*............ (*live*) in India. Chandra's mother and father ²............ (*grow*) rice, and Chandra had a job, too. She ³............ (*wash*) the Rajah's elephants. She ⁴............ (*look after*) the elephants very well. One day, the elephants were ill. Chandra was very sad. Their ears hurt. Then Chandra ⁵............ (*clean*) their ears, and the elephants were well again.

SEA GIRL AND THE GOLDEN KEY

7 Order the story by writing *1–7* in your notebook.

a .... A white bird tells Sea Girl about a key for a door.

b .... Sea Girl finds a key in a small brown box.

c ....*1*.... Sea Girl finds a lake on a mountain.

d .... The Dragon King's daughter and Sea Girl go to a cave.

e .... A red bird tells Sea Girl about the Dragon King's daughter.

f .... A blue bird tells Sea Girl that the Dragon King's daughter loves songs.

g .... Sea Girl sings, and a girl walks out of the lake.

8 **Write the correct words or phrases in your notebook.**

1 How **much / many** rice is there in the fields?

2 The villagers do not have **some / much** water.

3 "We haven't got **many / much** food," said Sea Girl's mother.

4 "We need **much / some** water," thought Sea Girl.

5 "There is **many / lots of** water in this lake," thought
Sea Girl.

Project work

1 The four "Adventurous Girls" meet in London. They
have to talk in English because they come from different
countries. Write a play script about their meeting. Then
act your play with some friends.

Tamasha:	Hi, I'm Tamasha.
Chandra:	Hello, I'm Chandra.
Tokoyo:	And I'm Tokoyo.
Sea Girl:	Hi, I'm Sea Girl. I'm from China.
Tamasha:	I'm from . . .

2 Choose one of the countries in the stories, and read about
it online. Make a poster about the country. Draw pictures
and maps, find photos, and write about the country.

3 Write a different ending for one of the stories. It can be a
happy ending or a sad ending.

An answer key for all questions and exercises can be found at
www.penguinreaders.co.uk

Glossary

adventurous (adj)
An *adventurous* person likes doing *dangerous* things.

bottom (n)
the opposite of "top". You can find many things at the *bottom* of the sea.

brave (adj)
A *brave* person is not *frightened*.

bring (v)
to take a thing to a person

confused (adj)
People who are *confused* do not understand things.

cry (v)
to speak loudly because you are angry or very happy

curse (n)
If someone puts a *curse* on you, bad things happen to you.

dangerous (adj)
A *dangerous* thing can *hurt* you. It is *dangerous* to stand near a fire.

double (v)
to make two of a thing. When you *double* two, you get four. When you *double* three, you get six.

down (prep)
You go *down* to the *bottom*, not up to the top.

fly away (phr v)
(past simple: **flew away**)
A bird *flies away* from one place to another place.

frightened (adj)
A person is *frightened* because a *dangerous* thing is near them.

greedy (adj)
A *greedy* person wants all the food or money.

grow (v)
(past simple: **grew**)
to get big

guard (n and v)
A *guard* stops people from
coming in to a place.

hold (v)
(past simple: **held**)
to have a thing in your hand

hurt (v)
You have an accident, and
then your body *hurts*.

idea (n)
when you think of a thing

ill (adj)
An *ill* person is not very well,
and their body *hurts*.

island (n)
A country, or part of a
country, with water on
every side of it.

look after (phr v)
to help a person or an animal

palace (n)
A *palace* is a big, beautiful
house.

throw (v)
to move your arm quickly
to move a thing

villager (n)
Villagers live in a village.

visit (v)
to go to a place and see the
people or the things there

voice (n)
A person speaks, and you
hear their *voice*.

worried (adj)
not happy because of
a *dangerous* thing or
a bad thing

Penguin Readers